Hannah's Treasure

LATTER-DAY DAUGHTERS

BOOKS IN THE LATTER-DAY DAUGHTERS SERIES

Hannah's
Treasure

LATTER-DAY DAUGHTERS

Launi K. Anderson

Published by
Deseret Book Company
Salt Lake City, Utah

To Jennifer, Paul, Richard, Susan, and Judy.
Hello? Hello? Where is everybody?

Library of Congress Cataloging-in-Publication Data

Anderson, Launi K., 1958–
   Hannah's treasure / by Launi K. Anderson.
     p.   cm. — (The Latter-day Daughters series)
   Summary: On a trip to Philadelphia in 1840 to sell the crops they
raised in the Blue Mountains, Hannah and her father meet a Mormon
preacher.
   ISBN 1-57345-297-1 (pb.)
   [1. Mountain life—Pennsylvania—Fiction. 2. Mormons—Fiction.
3. Pennsylvania—Fiction.] I. Title. II. Series.
PZ7.A54375Han   1997
[Fic]—dc20   96-20044
                                                  CIP
                                                  AC

Printed in the United States of America   8006-4589A

10 9 8 7 6 5 4 3 2

"Lay up for yourselves a treasure in heaven, yea, which is eternal, and which fadeth not away."

HELAMAN 5:8

CONTENTS

Prologue

A lot of people use up their lives fussing around, trying to make do for themselves, better than the next man. It don't matter none to Ma or Poppy— nor the rest of us—if we're poor as Job's turkey.* Poppy says, as long as *his own* are warm and dry, and have food on the table, well then, the blessings of heaven are his.

Ever since my ma's ma was a child, our folks been living here in these hills. We call them the Blue Mountains. Now, some may not think there's a dab of pride to be found in claiming that, but we know different. See, mountain folk are taught to work hard, be truthful, and take care of each other.

See the glossary at the end of this book for an explanation of unusual words and expressions marked with an asterisk (*).

We say our prayers and read from the Bible every night, before bedtime. And most important of all, we know to never leave off* thanking the Lord for his goodness.

Now, mind you, I'm not saying we're better or worse off than anybody else. It's just a fact to marvel, that rich folks never seem to see all the Lord has given them. When you don't have so much, it's a sight easier to keep track of your blessings.

CHAPTER ONE

Ramp Run

"Cally," I said, "you know Ma don't want you playing with mice."

"These ain't mice," she said. "These here are my babies."

"And just what would Saint Nicholas think if he saw those dirty things in your Christmas cradle?"

Six-year-old Cally put her hands on her hips. "He'd think I was a smart girl for finding my own dollies to play with, seeing as how *he* didn't leave me none. And anyway, they ain't dirty 'cause I just gave them a bath."

I peered into the doll bed at the half-dead critters. Cally had them wrapped tight in her white handkerchief. It made me nearly sick.

I tried to look stern. "Well, I'm tellin' *you*. Ma don't want you playing with no mice."

She stuck her nose in the air and scooted over till she had her back to me.

There was nothing to do but close the barn door behind me, and let her worry about her own self.

I heaved the last full bucket of milk out and set it next to the other four. Sophie and I had finished up the milking earlier than usual, but Poppy still wouldn't be happy with the news we brought.

My older sister came around the corner. We lugged one of the containers toward the house together.

"Sophie," I said, "why are we going to the trouble of hauling this to the porch if you say Poppy is just going to feed it to the hogs?"

"'Cause, it's for him to say, not us," she said. "He'll want to check it good before wasting it all."

"Couldn't he check it out here?"

"Hannah, you know Poppy doesn't ask us to take on more than our share. And it won't pain us to help him some. Mind what your doing now, you're sloshin'."

There's never any sense in arguing with Sophie,

but sometimes I do it, in spite of myself. She's a fair enough sister, I reckon. Even when she's scolding, her voice is soft and kind. But it's hard to set my mind to sharing the world with someone who is always right. Sophie can even get that stubborn little Cally to behave, when all she does is just stick up her nose at me.

Poppy was already standing on the porch stretching out a crick in his back when we came up to the side steps. He looked surprised—not to see us but rather that we brought a full milk bucket up to the house instead of packing it to cool by the river.

Sophie steered me toward the bottom step. With one last tug, we swung the bucket over and set it down. My shoulder ached, and I knew there was a blister starting on my carrying hand.

Poppy watched us for a moment, then said, "Your ma call up that milking,* girls?" He always talks kinda slow and steady. Like he's figuring the very best way of putting his words before letting them out.

"No, sir," Sophie said. "We thought you'd be wanting to look after this batch yourself, is all.

 Seems to me the cows found a fair patch of ramps.* The milk smells real nasty."

Poppy came down the steps and put three fingers into the white foam. He held his hand close to his nose and sniffed a few times. After touching one fingertip to his tongue, he made a face like he'd swallowed a tonic.*

"Well, that's a dadgum shame for your ma's butter churn. Though I expect the hogs will be after thanking you."

Sophie nodded. She was right again.

"Well, girls," Poppy said, "you saved your ma from a wasted day, all right. Ain't no one hungry for tainted* butter, or cheese neither."

"No sir," I said, wrinkling all up at the very idea.

Truth is that some folks around here eat ramps straight out of the ground. Some use them in soup, or fry 'em with fatback.* But we Ellisons never touch 'em. Not for a thing in this world.

Ma says, "Any man, child, or beast that's been eating ramps had better find himself a cave to sleep in, 'cause he ain't catching rest under this here roof."

"You girls will have to find the patch and root*
it out," Poppy said. "It must be in the south end
pasture somewhere. That's where they fed yesterday.
Finish your chores and I'll tell your ma to pack you
a lunch. Mind you're back long before supper,
whether you find those plants or not. I won't be
hunting you out at midnight."

"Yes, sir," Sophie and I said together.

We headed off to clean out the cow shed when I
remembered something.

"Poppy?" I called.

"What, girl?"

"Vassie and Lula. They got them each a split
hoof.*"

"That right?" he said, scratching at his chin
whiskers.

"Spotted them myself, just now. I thought you'd
want to know."

"Well, now, we'd better hold back an extra lug
of apples to store. Hadn't we? Hard winter coming.*"

I smiled 'cause I just knew he'd say that. I
turned to go but he called to me.

"Hannah?"

"Yes, Poppy?"

"Lord's blessed you with a keen eye, girl. You done good."

I skipped all the way to the barn with my insides all grinning and happy. Sophie'd already started raking the stalls out. I grabbed up a fork and tossed clean straw on the scratched-up ground. I love the smell of fresh hay. It takes my mind to Easter morning, even in October.

I know it ain't polite to brag on myself, but before I thought on it much, I said, "Sophie, Poppy said I have a keen eye. So what do you say to that?"

She waited a minute or two, then looked up and said, "I say that's right. You do have a keen eye. Isn't it you that takes up reading the Bible right off of my lap, when my eyes ache so bad? And isn't it you that threads all my stitching needles, when the candle burns low? If it weren't a sin to pine* on another, I'd wish to have eyes as good as yours."

I felt a flush of regret for saying what I did. "Sophie, I didn't mean nothing about your eyes. Why, they just need resting sometimes. They'll get better. Wait and see if they don't."

She smiled up at me. "I know you didn't mean nothing. It's all right. Besides, it won't take any eyes at all, to sniff out the ramp patch. But we better quit talking and finish up here. The chickens are hungry."

After breakfast, Ma said we'd be taking Cally along. As if we needed to worry about her too.

Sophie just took her hand and said, "She'll be all right, won't you, Cally?"

Cally looked up at me, smiling, and nodded. But I didn't trust her. We loaded up the lunch pails, a hoe, and a basket to carry back the ramp roots. Not that we wanted them or anything. We just needed Poppy to bury or burn 'em to keep the blamed cattle from running on to them again.

Any other time of year, Poppy would've fed ramps to the hogs, outright. But with it being fall, he couldn't run the risk of having the ham, lard, and all else tasting wild and nasty. Not just before slaughtering season.*

We led Effie, our most troublesome cow, up and over Blossom Hill toward the pasture. Cally had a squealing fit about halfway down, until we hoisted her onto Effie's back. Our hound dogs, Farish and Harley, stayed beside her, acting all fidgety like they were waiting for one of Effie's tricks. We brought along our naughtiest cow on purpose, figuring one of the sweeter, more gentle ones would've tried to behave while we were watching. That being the case, we thought they'd probably never lead us to the patch.

But we knew that Effie didn't care a lick. She'd just as soon eat the shingles off the roof as pasture grass, and she never cared who saw her do it. We hoped the wretched thing would take us right to the ramps.

Sure enough, as soon as I loosened my grip on her harness, she took off at a trot, lead rope flapping, with Cally hanging tight, screeching for all she was worth. The dogs ran with her steady, barking like they were coon hunting.*

"Hold on, Cally!" I hollered.

We tore after them, but that darn cow was fast. Effie galloped at such a pace that Cally's poor little head was just bobbing like a woodpecker.

"Maybe . . . we should scream . . . for her . . . to jump," I said, puffing like a steam kettle.

Sophie kept running but called back, "No! She'd get stomped on . . . for sure. Where . . . is that beast . . . going?"

"Look!" I said. "She's slowing down."

We rejoiced seeing that mean critter come to a

halt, but when we got closer, it was plain that Cally had got left behind somehow or other.

"Where is she?" Sophie said.

"Well, we couldn't have missed her, if she fell, that is. We'd a stepped right on her by now."

"Hannah, don't play. Cally! Where are you?"

Before Sophie could get too worked up, I grabbed Effie's halter and pulled hard. Coming around the side of her, I said, "Sophie, rest easy. Here she is."

There, plopped in the weeds, were the dogs, Farish and Harley, and a happy, dirty-faced Cally. That silly girl held a fistful of roots in each hand and sat chewing on them like they were summer carrots.

From five feet away, it was clear from the smell what we were up against. Sophie and I sank down in the grass. I sighed from deep down and shook my head. Looking sideways at each other, we said, "She found the ramps!"

CHAPTER TWO

Mountain Bounty

It took close to a week for Cally to sweeten up. Lucky for us, the weather was still warm enough that she could spend most of her days in the fresh air. Ma said that since we'd been the ones minding Cally* on "ramp day," wherever we went now, she was to tag along too. She was far too odorous* to be locked indoors next to anyone with a working sniffer. Outside, it wasn't so bad—as long as she didn't get too close or try breathing on us. And Ma didn't want her near baby Lark, for fear it would upset his constitution.*

By the second week in October, we were all busy sorting produce and supplies while Poppy packed up the extra to take to market in Philadelphia. We had more to spare this year than ever I could remember. We found a wagonload of nature's bounty, just after the last frost. From there the gathering went on clear till fall.

Way back last spring, as soon as the first frogs commenced to croaking, we'd spent a bit of our mornings hunting yarbs.* We gathered red sassafras—the bark, root, and leaves. Ma boiled the root to make blood tonic.* She dried the bark for candy, and we girls just chewed on the leaves like the cows do. We even dried a small pail of leaves to use later for thickening soup. Sassafras is so good for keeping folks well that Sophie and I made up a song about it:

In the spring of the year when the blood is
    too thick,
There's nothing so fine as a sassafras stick.
It tones up the liver and strengthens the
    heart,
And to the whole body new life does
    impart.

We found fresh poke* that Ma fried up for supper with bacon grease and ham. Cally gave us a bad scare back then by stuffing a handful of the berries in her mouth. Sophie told her that she'd be wearing angel wings within the hour if she swallowed them. Finally, we got her to spit 'em out. They mostly landed in the dirt, but a few hit my dress like a nosebleed. Poke berries, besides being poison, make a fine dark red dye.

By midyear, after the first new moon* appeared, Poppy took to robbing* the beehives on the edge of the orchard. First he put on thick clothes, then set

fire to a bundle of rags and dead twigs. He held the smoky twists* right near the hives to make the bees sleepy. With a hot knife he cut and lifted chunks of honeycomb* out and quickly packed it in jars, comb and all. He's real careful to leave enough honey behind so the newborn bees don't starve to death come winter.

None of us are too keen on helping with the bees. We're far too fearful of getting stung. Poppy says that's something you can always count on. He only talks that way 'cause he's brave and a bee sting doesn't scare him none.

Once, we girls set out to eat our lunches near the back woods. Cally made her own sandwich that day. The honey was just wasting out the sides of the bread and running down her arms. She didn't seem to mind much until the bees came after her 'cause she smelled so good and sweet.

If a bee is just curious, the best advice is to stay still. If you are holding onto something they're after, I'd say to drop it. But if what they want is sticking to your arms, and face, and dress, well then, what you want to do is hightail it out of there and hope they don't beat you home. It was sure hard not to laugh watching Cally run like the bull got loose. I guess she made it.

Because our swarms take nectar from both apple blossoms and the shrubs nearby, folks all over Pennsylvania say that Ellison honey beats all else. The real secret, Poppy says, is the sourwood* trees that line the orchard. Bees love those blossoms better than anything. The flavor they lend to a recipe makes the whole tree well respected in these parts. In fact, if ever an old limb dies, it will be crafted into stout, useful things like tool handles, sled runners, or bedposts. One thing's for sure. You won't catch us using any part of it for common firewood. That could bring on terrible bad luck, maybe even a family disaster.

Early in August, after each warm rain spell, we

gathered morel* from under the apple trees. We hung them by twine, to dry in the woodshed. Ma says they give a special flavor to any stew or soup they're put with. We use them all winter long.

Later, chestnuts fell so plentiful, we could hardly take a step into the forest without crushing a fistful of them with our feet. We made a game of scooping them into baskets to haul home, and Cally was convinced that she was having a powerful, big time.*

By mid-September, the apples came on* full, and even Ma ventured out to help us pick, as long as the baby was sleeping.

We filled almost three huge baskets from each tree. It was our best crop ever. Why, even back when Poppy split the work with Uncle Wade we never knew such a bounty.

"Unexpected gift from the Lord," Poppy said.

Now, since Uncle Wade moved from these parts, the plowing, planting, hives, and orchards are ours to tend to and sell from.

Still, Poppy always says, "I've never fussed about sharing the farm, as long as I'm sharing the labor besides. And to work alongside kin* is a true blessing."

I sometimes wish that baby Lark had of been born before Sophie and me. By now, he'd be sharpening axes, felling* trees, and hunting meat with his own flintlock,* right alongside Poppy.

We know Poppy could use more help, but in these parts, girls are expected to stay near the cabin and learn home tasks, like milking, soap and candle making, weaving, cooking, spinning, and grinding corn. Now and again, though, Poppy gets to needing us almost like we were boys. We do all we can, but the heavy labor still falls pretty much on him. It's my notion that he sorely misses his brother.

We woke up early one morning without a rousing* from Ma. The goose-feather quilt was cozy and warm, but no bed will ever be big enough when Cally and her cold feet are on the same mattress.

I lay staring into the darkness, then said, "Sophie? Who do you think Poppy will choose to go with him?"

"Can't know," Sophie whispered. "Said he'd decide by sunup. I suppose we have near ten minutes for that."

"I say he'd be wise to take you."

"How's that?" she asked.

"Well, the way I see it, since you're the oldest,

17

and *none* of us have gone much past the valley, by rights it should be you first."

"I don't know that Ma or Poppy will pay any mind to that. Though I'd love to go. Think of it . . . ," she said, with her voice all dreamy-like. "The city. Fancy ladies, wearing hats and gloves, hanging on the arms of fine gentlemen. I'd probably act like a fool just staring at them."

That was truly something I couldn't picture. Sophie acting like a fool, for any reason. I knew she wanted this trip, and deep inside my own wishing heart, part of me was hoping Poppy *would* choose her. But then again, it *was* the city.

Suddenly, a steady thumping from below our bed shook us wide awake.

"Come on, Hannah," Sophie said. "That's Ma's broom calling us. We better climb down before it wakes Cally."

We threw our clothes on as best we could. It took a minute till our eyes fixed, to see right in the dark. I could feel my body starting to shiver as I pulled on my chilled frock. Being in such a hurry to hear Poppy's answer, I tucked my hair under my mobcap,* hoping no one would pay any mind that I hadn't brushed it a stroke.

When I turned to make my way down the ladder, there stood Sophie with her hands on her hips.

"Hannah Patrice Ellison," she sounded serious, but her lips looked ready to curl up in a smile. "Do you figure on trying to fool Ma that way? Shame on you."

I untied my cap and took up the brush.

Looking pleasured that I was minding her, she started for the stairs. As she disappeared into the main room, I jerked the brush down through my hair three or four times.

"That should do it," I said to myself. I looked at my sleepy, ice-footed sister still making a faint snoring sound in the warm bed. She looked almost sweet.

"A load of cannon fire wouldn't wake that girl," I said low.

CHAPTER THREE

Growing Up

"Oh, Lord," Poppy prayed, "look down on this family with mercy. We thank you for the gravy and biscuits that we eat this very morning. Bless us that we'll live to find your truth and feel peace and contentment on that day. We thank you for your love and grace. In Jesus' name. Amen."

"I'm dreadful sorry, Sophie," I whispered. "I never thought he'd choose *me*."

She nodded slightly but didn't speak a word.

I turned toward the head of the table. Ma and Poppy were talking about the Bible verses they'd read last night.

"I've always pondered that one," Poppy said. "It's clear the Lord uses apostles and prophets to teach his word. I ask every preacher I meet about that. Seems they don't believe it themselves."

Ma nodded. "But how do they dare not to believe? It says it, right here in Ephesians 4:11."

My pa shook his head. "Don't rightly know."

"Maybe the full truth isn't to be found these days," Ma said. "But we'll keep on praying and the Lord will guide us."

I waited politely for a place to speak. Usually young'uns are expected to be quiet at the table. Our Poppy has never whupped us for talking, like some folks do their children. Even if he frowned at me, I knew he'd still listen.

As he and Ma each took a bite of biscuit, I cleared my throat and said, "Poppy, wouldn't it be a wiser choice to take Sophie instead of me?"

Poppy looked into my face for a while, like he does, then finally said, "Hannah, it ain't different from what I told you already. Ma's fixing to spin and weave the flax* while we're gone. Jake Jackson's bringing the loom next week. Sophie's got to learn it, and now's her chance."

Ma looked at me real serious. "Your pa and I sense that soon there'll be a wagonload of young men courting your sister. She's nigh on to thirteen years. Why, I married your pa the winter after my fourteenth birthday. Now, just how shamed would we be, if our eldest couldn't spin or weave? Tell me."

"Mighty, I expect," I said softly.

"That's right," Ma said. "Law, any man will find treasure sure in making one of our girls his wife. But when he comes in from a long day, he needs to know that his bride can care for a household."

"Hannah," Poppy said, "you thinking you don't want to come?"

"Oh, no, Poppy. It ain't that." I turned to Sophie. She sat with her head down, embarrassed at us talking about her in such ways. "I just can't bear to see Sophie so mournful."

My sister put her hand on my arm. "I'm fine, Hannah. Truly, I am," she said.

Ma smiled at Sophie and me. "Your pa and I say, what with the bounty this year, you girls are welcome to sell your own goods. And you can do as you please with the money. Hannah, could be you'll find something to bring back from the city for both your sisters. They'll know it's a treasure."

"Poppy?" I said. "What will you do with all *your* money?"

He looked at Ma. She nodded.

"Well," he said, "your ma and me been thinking

for awhile now about building up this house. Lark will need his own bed soon, and we're already stepping over one another. We figure four rooms instead of two should do us fine.

"Of a certain," Ma said, "we'll need the regular supplies—flour, sugar, and salt. But we'll buy nails too. We're looking for enough left over for hiring Toddy Burton's boy to help your pa build, come spring."

"Four rooms!" I said, clapping my hands. "Just think of it."

Ma smiled over at Pa and said, "I'd like to see you get yourself a watch. You've been telling time with the sun for long enough now."

Poppy slapped the table. "There now. You see? Everything will be all right. Now, if you don't mind, I'm gonna eat. I'm clean wore out from all this talking."

I looked at Sophie, and she broke into a smile. I decided then and there to bring her back something real good, and Ma too.

Cally sat staring at us both. When she looked full toward me, she grinned big and crossed her eyes. Sophie and I couldn't help giggling. I think I'll bring Cally back a grasp of bitterroot.*

CHAPTER FOUR

Cold Feet

After our regular chores, we girls, even Cally, sat round the table stringing up* apple rings* and pumpkin to dry by the fireplace. That way we'd have them to eat through winter.

Ma planned to press cider* and make apple butter* all week. But she couldn't start until we finished sorting the eating apples from the wormy ones. Poppy and I would be taking the very best into town to sell.

By the time our work was hung up in rows, my fingers were poked and sore. I was ready for new chores. Ma figured since we cut the sassafras bark, we could help her make the candy. I worked the dried bark over the tin grater* until my fingers came close to being shaved. Next, it was simmered, strained, and mixed into boiled-down sugar. Ma poured it into three pans. When it hardened, we broke it into small pieces. One pan was saved for us, and the others we shook in an empty flour sack. That way, it wouldn't stick together. We'd sell it too.

By week's end we had the root vegetables buried,* honey and sassafras candy to sell, turnips, potatoes, and apples bagged, chestnuts sacked, morel ropes tied up, and honey jars ready to pack.

Everybody stood outside watching Poppy tie down the canvas over the loaded wagonbed. We'd be leaving tomorrow morning first thing after breakfast.

"Come inside, Hannah," Ma said. "With the loading done, we'll work on getting you packed."

Cally tugged on Ma's skirt. "Is Hannah getting stored up in an apple bag too?"

Ma laughed. "No, baby. We're gonna let her ride up there beside your pa. I'm saying that we need to get her clothes and such ready for the trip."

"What trip?" Cally wailed. "I want to go on a trip!"

She kept on like that all the while we were packing, until Poppy got fed up and hauled her outside.

Into a knapsack we folded my one other linen dress, a pair of wool drawers,* an extra shift,* my clean white pinafore, and a linsey-woolsey* bonnet. We set my shoes on top of the pile and left out my wrapping cloak* to use as a lap robe in the morning.

Sophie let me take the hairbrush, saying, "I'll just share Ma's. But mind you use this, now." She smiled. "Can't have the city folks wondering about your upbringing."*

Poppy climbed the ladder carrying Cally, asleep on his shoulder. He put her down in the middle of the mattress. She rolled over, wrapping the entire quilt around herself in one turn.

Ma and Poppy looked to me, then Sophie, and started laughing.

"Seems you two may be in for a chilly night," Poppy said. "We all have plenty to do tomorrow, so we better be blowing the candle out on this day." He bent down and kissed Cally's head, then Sophie's, then mine. "Get your sleep."

Ma hugged us each. "I love you, girls," she said. "Sleep good."

After climbing into our bed and yanking back a piece of the quilt, I said, "Sophie?"

"Yeah?"

"Are you still feeling sad about not going with Poppy?"

"No, I've settled my mind to it. I want you to go and have a big time."

"I'd have more fun if you were coming. Fact is, I'm kinda scared."

"You know there's nothing to worry about. But I'll miss you too. Anyway, Ma's right. I do need to learn to work cloth, so it's a sacrifice I should be happy to make.

"What do you mean . . . sacrifice?" I said.

"When a person does without something they want or need real bad, because they're trying to do what's right, or to help someone else. That's a sacrifice. But Hannah, the peculiar thing is, when you give that something up, it doesn't pain you like you expect. Somehow, it feels good. You just trust the Lord to get you by. And suppose my eyes were to get worse. . . ."

"They won't," I said loud enough to stir Cally. "I just know your eyes will get better."

"Shhhh," she said. "Hannah, it'll be all right, however which way it goes. What I was about to say was, if my eyes do grow worse, and I've already learned how to spin and weave, maybe I could still do it. I figure on practicing now and again with my eyes closed until I sort it out."

I wanted to say, "You're the best sister and the bravest person I know." But all that came out was, "I love you, Sophie."

"I love you too, Hannah."

Just then, Cally flipped over and snuggled closer to me. I felt a shock like lightning that took my breath away.

Sophie said, "What is it, Hannah?"

I scrunched over closer to the edge of the bed, saying, "Oh, nothing. I just met up with Miss Frosty Feet. That's all."

CHAPTER FIVE

To Market, to Market

We made our way steadily down the worn-out road, heading toward a pink, just-before-dawn sky. The valley below us was barely starting to split shadows into color. I pulled the cloak up around my shoulders and set the pan of warm pumpkin bread on my lap. At first it had been too hot to touch, but now, after riding for close to an hour, it had cooled down enough to keep my legs warm.

Poppy didn't talk much but only whistled now and then to Farish. It called him back from running too far.

Me being all snugly wrapped like I was, it was a hardship to stay awake. I kept thinking that if I really tottered off to sleep, I might could fall clean out of the wagon and roll away altogether. And how would it do to wake up alone in some grassy place,

and be left to either follow Poppy's trail somehow
or make my own way home? That idea snapped my
eyes open more than once.

I'd nearly wore out Ma's face in my mind,
thinking of her kissing me good-bye, standing by
the porch, with Sophie waving till we were out of
sight. I laughed to myself thinking of sleepy Cally,
leaning out the bedroom window to watch us go. I
about took a stroke* when she hollered, "Bye-bye,"
and came close to toppling right out. If she hadn't
caught the deerskin cover,* she'd of landed in the
woodpile, most likely on her head. That child does
keep our hearts pounding, I can say that.

By noon, we had already forged one river and
were coming up on the far half of the Cumberland
Valley. Poppy asked me if I was ready to stop for
lunch. We'd nearly picked the pumpkin bread to
bits, but I figured we could just eat lunch and keep
right on riding.

Poppy laughed. "What's your hurry, girl? We
need to rest the animals and stretch our weary
bones."

I knew he was right. My muscles were jostled
sore and I was getting tired of sitting. It felt pleas-
ing to think that if we didn't stop we'd arrive in

Philadelphia sooner. But Poppy reminded me that we'd be delayed considerably if we worked both horses to death. I decided to be patient and let old Jack and Nessie chew on meadow grass for awhile, and leave them be.

We ate the crackling bread,* cushaw pie,* and apples Ma packed for us. The whole meal tasted fine. We knew that when the fresh food was gone, we'd be feasting on dock seeds,* dried beef, and whatever Poppy hunted along the way. Thinking on that caused us to eat Ma's cooking real slow.

By the time we were ready to get back on the road old Jack and Nessie were prancing around like they had somewhere to be. It was all Poppy could do to keep them from taking off before we got settled in the wagon.

We reached the top of a small hill just as the sun was heading down. Poppy found a cozy stopping place in a clearing surrounded by birch trees. He built a fire, while I set up camp. We ate the same fixin's we'd had for lunch. Only this time Poppy whittled a couple of sticks to a point and roasted corn over the fire. It was awful good and filled us right up.

I made my bed under the wagon, my pa took a place close to the fire, and old Farish wandered around for a while. Poppy and I kept warm with ram hides beneath us and each in our own bedroll.

Once we were asleep, Farish thought sure he needed to lay down right next to me. That worked well enough at the beginning, 'cause he gave off warmth. But before long, he started running after every night noise* that sang out. Each time he heard an owl or something, he'd dash from under the wagon, like his tail was snakebit. He roamed the forest with the look of a wild creature, chasing and barking at what he couldn't catch.

I never heard him come back, but a few hours later, something moved near the edge of the woods, and Farish lit out again. Only this time, he tried to hop right over me. Being in such a rush, that blamed dog planted one foot in my stomach on his way out. I raised up hard to catch my breath and cracked my head on the boards above me.

"Ow!" I hollered. "You rotten thing."

Poppy sat up staring at me as I held my middle with one hand and rubbed my forehead with the other.

"Hannah, what's all this commotion?"

"Sorry, Poppy. It was just old Farish, bounding out of here yapping and howling like he was on fire. I could swear I been gut-shot and hit with a shovel at the same time."

Poppy looked like he was aiming to laugh, but said, "Up, girl. Let me look at your head."

I crawled out and stood beside him. He took a hold of my chin and turned my face toward the moonlight. "Hmmmm," he said. "That's a fair bump. Small cut too. I can fix it. Your innards all right?" I nodded and sat down on a rock. Poppy fetched the strawbag* from the food box and whistled for Farish. I watched him crack an egg onto the ground as the dog bolted up and licked away every drop. Next, my pa peeled back the shell and tore a bit of the egg-skin away. He cleaned my forehead with a kerchief dipped in water, then dried it with his sleeve. I stood real still while he carefully set the egg-skin over the tiny cut and dabbed at it with his fingers.

"Now, then," he said, looking hard at his work, "that'll stop the bleeding and tighten the split."

I wanted to reach up and feel the bump, but I knew better. I smiled and said, "Thank you, Poppy."

We rested easy for the few hours of night left to us. It was peaceful only on account of Poppy roping Farish to a lind* tree. At least that crazy dog wised up and didn't make another sound till daybreak.

CHAPTER SIX

River Crossing

One day about mid-morning, we came within sight of the mighty Susquehanna River. Near took my breath away, being so big and blue. Sitting on a hill, looking down on it, we ate our breakfast.

"Fried squirrel is about as good a eating as the country provides," my pa said. "Wouldn't you say, Hannah?"

I nodded, savoring every bite. "And what I wouldn't trade for a potful of Ma's dumplings, about now."

Poppy just smiled and kept eating.

Autumn had settled down fast and turned every tired, green thing a bright orange, yellow, or scarlet. The river valley lay out ahead of us like a gigantic patch quilt, nestled over the land. It made me think of home.

I thought about Cally looking after the chickens for the first time, and wondered if she'd get fidgety and pour the seed out in one big pile, instead of taking the time to spread it like she ought.

My mind went to Sophie, sitting at the spinning wheel, turning flax into thread. Then, as I closed my eyes, I could almost see her working Jake Jackson's loom, with Ma standing by.

I felt a heavy pain inside my heart, like I'd swallowed a turnip whole, and it stuck somewhere. About now, Ma'd be finishing up the cider. The apple butter would be setting in jars, sealed up for winter with waxed rags.* Why, some of my earliest recollections are of sitting on a chair, watching Ma do her fall chores, stirring preserves, grinding corn, or weaving cloth.

I swallowed, but the lump only seemed to grow bigger. In all my ten autumns, I've been right there, beside Ma and Sophie. How troublesome to know everything was happening the same as ever, only without me. I was so far away.

I felt Poppy's hand on my shoulder, his fingers squeezing softly. It wasn't till I turned and looked up into his tan, work-worn face that I realized I was crying. It was a peculiar cry, though. Part of it was sad, like a sold pup, for missing Ma, Sophie, the baby, and even Cally. But the other part was joyful, and excited to be right here, on this very hill, seeing the world with my pa.

I reached down and took a hold of his hand and wiped my face with the back of my arm. We walked over to hitch up the horses together. He never said nothing about my bawling, but he seemed to understand.

I walked beside the wagon all the way down to the river. We waited at the bank for over an hour till a long, wooden raft, with mules, wagons, and people in it, came floating toward us. This thing was bigger than our entire cornfield, I knew that. My pa pointed out two men working poles that sunk down into the water.

"Those men best jump," I said, "before they wash down."

Poppy threw back his head and laughed. "Hannah, that there's called a flatboat.* They'll see us waiting here and work on over to give us a ride."

"A ride!" I said. "Poppy, I don't want no ride in

a big floating box. It'll sink for sure. Couldn't we just go around this old river?"

"Afraid not, child. This is our way across, so get ready to climb on when it gets here." My pa whistled for Farish to hop into the wagon seat while he held the horses still.

I couldn't figure for the life of me how any man could stop that thing. But as it got closer, it did slow down, and it came to rest a horse-length from where we stood. My mouth was hanging open, 'cause I'd never seen anything like it in all my days. I couldn't tell which I was feeling most, afraid or amazed. All I do know for sure is that Poppy got the wagon, the horses, and the hound onto this box without my paying him any mind. Then, before I could draw breath to holler, he scooped me up like a new calf and set me in the middle of it. I saw there was no chance of jumping off without killing myself outright, so I climbed into the wagon next to Farish and hung onto his collar. I felt a touch better knowing that dogs can swim. My pa stood near the men who were trying to row this boat. I heard them say that they float travelers up and down the river all year long till the water freezes. They pick up whoever is waiting on the banks and take them across, or down, whichever way they want.

I tried acting calm when everyone turned to look at me. Poppy said something low to the boatmen, then smiled at me. I figured he was saying that this was my first ride of this sort.

As we rounded a bend in the river, there came a faint whistling sound from the shore. Here the river's edge was covered in brush and trees, so it was hard to say where the noise came from. Just when I'd decided it was only a bird, two men in fancy suit coats came bursting through the trees. They ran along the bank ahead of us, waving their arms and shouting, "Ho, there! Pull off!* Wait!" and the like.

Poppy helped the boatmen work the guide pole* so the raft would heave to one side. I thought sure we'd all be thrown over, or the timbers would crack up, and I fixed my mind not to watch it happen. Jerking loose a corner of the wagon canvas, I hid between a stack of honey crates and an apple sack. My thinking was that being flattened under our own farm goods would be better than washing downstream in some foreign river and never being seen again. I told myself not to peek from under the canvas, but my eyes did it by their own self.

With such short warning to come to shore, we didn't truly stop until the boat was quite a ways past the trees. The two men ran and hopped on, laughing, slapping backs, and shaking hands with the rowers.

The strangers seemed pleasant enough, though one acted more sober and the other smiled and joked with everyone like they were family. I wasn't sure how Poppy would take to them, on account of him being so quiet and the one stranger chattering like a magpie. So I watched them closely.

I could see they were tired and a bit dusty, but their clothes and shoes looked store made. Poppy always wore his hair long and curling on his shoulders, like the rest of the men back home. But both of these travelers had their hair combed back, with a curl flipping up on one side.

"City gentlemen," I whispered to myself. I couldn't wait to tell Sophie.

They talked about their travels and where they'd been. Said they were bound for a somewhere called Jerusalem. Now, I've heard of a Jerusalem in the Bible, but I can't know if it's the same place.

Poppy sat rubbing his chin whiskers, looking

real thoughtful, like he does. They told him of some great mission they were doing for the Lord.

When the one man asked where my pa was heading, to my surprise, Poppy not only *told them,* but went on with what we were taking to market, how good our crops had been, and all else about our family. Why, I'd never heard him talk such a blue streak* in all my life, and to strangers, at that. None of us Ellisons are too keen on strangers.

Before he'd taken much of a breath, Poppy tossed back the tail end of the wagon cover. I was still hid, but I knew he saw me. He showed them our goods and offered them a small sack of apples to take along on their journey.

The smiling man put a hand on my pa's shoulder and said, "We have no money to pay for such a gift, my friend."

"Then I reckon you can think on it as that," Poppy said, "a gift." He shook hands with both strangers as the boatmen eased up to the far shore.

It didn't take a wink* to get us back on dry ground—wagon, horses, hound dog, and all. Poppy got up onto his seat and took the reins. He waved and shouted, "Thank you kindly," as the boat slipped out into the moving water again.

"You can come out, Hannah," Poppy said. "We made it, sure enough!"

Climbing into my place, I said, "Did you know those men, Poppy? You sure talked to 'em like you did."

"I couldn't stop myself. They said their names were Elder Page and Elder Hyde. There sure was something about 'em. I could feel it."

I looked over at Poppy and wondered.

CHAPTER SEVEN

Treasure Hunt

After eight days of rabbit stew, ashcake,* and cornmeal mush, we came to a place overlooking the city itself. It was a sight so wondrous, I couldn't leave off staring.

Poppy said, "Well, girl, there it is. Philadelphia. It's time to put your shoes on."

The city stretched out ahead of us, about two miles away, pleading for us to hurry on. Poppy and I scrubbed at the last creek we crossed, so we would look presentable. We hunted out my shoepacs* and filled them with dry leaves. When I set my feet in 'em, it was real scratchy at first. But before too long, my toes cozied up, nice and warm.

It felt like heaven above to put on a clean shift and dress after such a long trip. I'd worn my bonnet a few mornings when the sun was high. Since it was spoiled* now, I tied on my cap. But then, remembering Sophie's last advice to me, I took it off again and brushed through my hair. *Twenty-five* strokes, this time.

"Ready?" Poppy asked.

The excitement shivered through me like a fright. I took a deep breath and nodded.

He whistled for Farish, clicked to the horses, and off we went. All along, we'd traveled on narrow roads, rocky roads, and sometimes no roads at all. But as we came nearer to the crowded city, the small path behind us widened out to the size of Dog Tooth Creek. Well, pretty near.

Poppy pinched back* the horses so they wouldn't get all wild, being next to this many people. I just sat there, turning my head this way and that way so's not to miss nothing. Poppy kept smiling down at me.

The stores and buildings stood so close together that one of Cally's mice babies couldn't have squeaked between them. And some had two or three stacked right on top of each other. And the noise! I couldn't imagine such a commotion, even if every critter at our place commenced to bawling at the same time.

44

Before I'd had enough of gawking, we came to a stop in front of a white building.

"What's this place?" I asked.

Poppy got out, stretched and yawned big, then patted old Jack's neck, saying, "Hotel and Mercantile."

"Oh," I said, still trying to figure out what that meant.

"This is where we'll be staying, girl, and selling our goods."

I hopped down from the wagon while Poppy tied the horses and called Farish to the front. Pressing my face against the left window, I tried to sniff the baked goods sitting there like a harvest festival. Nothing.

But inside, the store had so many smells mixing together, it was hard to sort out what was what. The scents of wood, leather, grains, spices, molasses, cheese, and vegetables all swirled around in the air.

A lady with fawn-colored hair curling around her face came from the back room and stood behind the counter. Her dress was right simple next to the other women outside. It made me take to* her right off. I fancied* the way the little crinkles around her eyes seemed to smile along with the rest of her face.

"So, Mr. Ellison," she said, "has it been a year already?"

Poppy pulled off his hat and nodded. "Yes, ma'am."

"It's a pleasure to see you again. The crops have done well, I trust?"

Another nod.

Then turning to me, she said, "And your daughter is lovely." Coming around closer, she said, "I'm Lottie Dalton. Folks around here call me Mrs. Lottie."

I'd never called an older person by their given name, in all my life. Glancing to Poppy, I knew he was saying no, with his eyes.

"And what might your name be, dear?"

"Hannah Patrice Ellison, ma'am."

I reckon there was something polite I was supposed to do but didn't know what, so I just kept still.

"Well, Hannah, what do you think of your first time in the city?"

Grinning, I said, "It's mighty big. I didn't know there was so many people in the wide world."

She and my pa both laughed. Then, touching my hair, she said, "You feel free to look around. I'll

46

be working with your pa for a while. If you have any questions, by all means, ask."

She and Poppy went to the front counter while I walked slowly up and down the rows of shelves and tables. On one aisle was all sorts of men things—boots, bridles, tools, and knives. Down another, anything a lady could think of, and a thousand that she couldn't. Teapots, iron pans, washtubs, buttons, and needles. I stared closely at a table full of kitchen tools. I knew what some were, by sight. The kneading boards, rolling pins, and mush sticks were things my ma used back home. Other things I read the signs for. I had about made up my mind to bring Mama home a maple potato pounder* when I rounded the corner and found something perfect.

On a shelf marked "Fancy Goods," together with china vases, teacups, and hairbrushes, sat a looking glass* made of silver metal. The handle and back were carved up with swirls and tiny flowers. I thought, if Ma had *that* to see in, she'd know for sure how pretty she was.

On the list in my mind, I put "Ma—looking glass."

Perched atop a high ledge sat six china dolls, with painted eyes and real hair. I thought of Cally and her Christmas cradle. But those dolls were too fancy for a six-year-old, and no doubt, too dear.*

Lower down, spread across a plank shelf, lay five or six pairs of knit stockings in different colors. *This* got me thinking of Cally and her icy feet. I knew right then I'd found what that girl needed. Just as I was fixing to put the dark brown ones on my "list," my eyes caught sight of something else.

Off to the side, half-covered by a set of crockery  bowls, was a little rag doll. It was a sorry-looking thing that seemed to be hollering out for love. Her wool hair stuck up in places, like mine does before a brushing. I wanted to pick the poor dolly up and hold her, but I knew not to.

I thought of the list again. Heaving a sigh, I decided, "Cally—rag doll."

I knew baby Lark was too tiny to care, so that left only Sophie to choose for.

Poppy was working hard bringing in our sacks, barrels, and crates. Mrs. Dalton stood quietly writing it all up for him.

"Hannah," Poppy called. He set down the box that held all our goods, Sophie's and mine. "Mrs. Dalton's pretty-near done figuring my sum. Come show her what you brought, so's she can add it up."

I walked forward and hefted out the bags of chestnuts, and handed them to Mrs. Dalton. Next, I lifted the morel ropes and laid them on the counter. Lastly, I brought up the sack of candy. Mrs. Dalton peered into the bag and looked at me. Her face was beaming.

"Sassafras," she said. "My favorite! I may have to keep this for myself."

I put my head down, smiling. "There's honey candy in that bag too, ma'am."

"Wonderful! Nuts, mushrooms, and candy. You've both had a splendid year, it seems. Now, dear, did you want cash or credit for your goods?"

I looked at Poppy for help, but he was too busy holding the pocket watches up to his ear, then to the light.

"There's folks back home," I said, "waiting on me, to see what I bring 'em. I'm nearly through choosing."

Mrs. Dalton raised her eyebrows. "Ah, credit then."

Scrunching up my face, I said, "But for my sister Sophie—she's twelve—she might could use the stitching needles over there, except . . ." I leaned over to whisper, "she don't see so good sometimes. 'Specially tiny things. I'd hate to cause her sorrow over it."

Mrs. Dalton thought for a moment, then snapped her fingers. "You know, I just may have the perfect gift." Reaching down behind the counter she brought up a rounded piece of glass with a wooden handle attached. I took it and saw that everything behind it changed from small to big.

"It's called a magnifier," she said.

"Will this make *everything* look bigger? Like Bible reading, or needle eyes, or stitching?"

"Well, yes, dear. Whatever it's in front of."

"Just right," I said. Then on my list I checked off "Sophie—magnifier."

I walked through the store pointing out the other things for my family, while Mrs. Dalton collected them up. When I was done, she gave me a funny look.

"Aren't you getting something for yourself, dear?" she asked.

I hadn't thought of that. It didn't take my eyes one sweep over the store to see the stockings again. In a way, I thought, they *would* be for me.

"If I have enough left, I'd sure like to get those," I said, pointing to the dark brown pair.

"Fine enough," she said.

Mrs. Dalton wrapped my treasures in brown paper and gave me six coins besides. I clutched the parcel to me feeling like I would bust with joy.

Poppy decided on the watch he wanted and handed it over. Mrs. Dalton did some more figuring, then gave the timepiece back. Poppy smiled at me and slid it into his shirt pocket. I think he felt silly finally getting something for himself.

For the apples, honey, and all else we brought, he took the rest of his pay in cash money. As he poured the coins into his leather pouch, I saw that a good many of them were shiny gold.

CHAPTER EIGHT

Philadelphia

"Ain't you gonna get the supplies yet, Poppy?"

"Salt, flour, and sugar can wait till morning," he said.

"And nails." I laughed. "Don't be forgetting the nails."

"*And nails.* I won't forget."

We followed Mrs. Dalton up the stairs to our room. After unlocking the door, she motioned for us to go on in. It was a right pretty place. On each side wall stood a beautiful, dark wood bed with tall, polished posts. A small table and lamp took up the middle of the floor. Best of all, the room had a window overlooking the city. From where we stood, we could see the people buzzing around below us like a swarm of Poppy's bees.

"It's quarter past four now," Mrs. Dalton said.

"You have plenty of time to get settled and even see some of our city. Try to be back by eight. Dinner will be served then."

After she closed the door, I twirled around twice, letting my dress flutter about my legs.

"The city!" I sang. "Can we go see it now, Poppy—now, before nightfall? We can rest later. Please?"

He sat still on the edge of the bed for a few minutes before curling into a smile and nodding.

I jumped up toward him and tossed my arms around his neck. "Oh, thank you! Thank you!"

Out on the street, people hurried past us from every direction. A good many folks looked just as Sophie said they would, all fixed and fancy like they were scurrying to a party. Many of the dresses were fashioned in spring colors, and doozied up with lace and buttons.

Some ladies, as pretty as they were, still gave me cause to wonder. It seemed that the top half of 'em was willow thin, especially towards the middle. But the further down my eyes went, the bigger the women got. Why, I even fretted over the poor horses that had to tow such large-ended ladies*

around town. When I asked Poppy about it, he only said, "I ain't figured that one out my own self. Best leave it alone."

I suppose they eat fine in Philadelphia.

As we headed down the wooden sidewalks, I thought my eyes would pop right out of my head. Every building stored a whole different load of goods. The first one we got to had all kinds of meat, poultry, and even fish hanging in one window. Another store had stacks of leather boots everywhere, and near a hundred belts curled up or hooked on wall pegs.

I heard music, laughter, and yelling all at one time, coming from a place Poppy called a saloon. He aimed to scoot me full chisel* past that one.

Finally at the end of one street we came to a store with a sign reading "Confectioner." To my utter joy, Poppy turned and went inside. A strong scent of mint came at us the second we opened the door, making my eyes water a bit.

Inside a glass counter sat rows of china plates and bowls filled with little stacks of sweets. With our candy from home looking like it did, I couldn't guess how the fudge, taffy balls, and pralines ended up all the same size. Some had tiny sugar flowers or bows set on top, and everything looked too pretty to eat.

Poppy poked a finger toward a bowl marked "Peanut Brittle" and the lady started gathering a few pieces into a tiny sack.

"How about you, Hannah?" he said. "What'll you have?"

I knew without thinking at all. "A chunk of fudge, please," I said. We waited till we got outside to take our first bite. Poppy crunched down hard on his brittle, while I bit into a creamy, dark square of heaven itself. I closed my eyes so my tongue couldn't do nothing but taste the sweet chocolate stirring in my mouth. The worst thing about fudge is making yourself let go and swallow.

Up the road a ways, a crowd had begun to gather. In the center stood a man with his back to us. It looked to me like he was giving a speech. He spoke in a loud enough voice, but with his back to us it was hard to make out most of the words.

Poppy steered us closer to the swarm of people. I noticed right off that plenty of the folks here looked like farmers. The fine-dressed people didn't look interested.

"Some kind of preacher, I reckon," Poppy said, stepping nearer. "Let's hold up and see what he has to say." We Ellisons have always been respectful of preachers.

As we wiggled in further, I thought I'd heard the voice before. Poppy must have felt something too, 'cause he stopped and tilted his head like Harley and Farish do when they're listening hard. I was more taken with the look on Poppy's face than anything the preacher was saying.

Poppy said, "That's *him,*" like he was talking to himself.

"Who?" I asked. But he didn't hear me. Something this man was talking about had sure caught a grip on my pa. He stood looking like there was a spell come over him. 'Cept we don't believe in spells.

"Poppy, who is it?" I said again.

He put his finger to his lips to hush me. A few people walked away, laughing. That eased up the crowd enough that Poppy could move in closer. Just then, the preacher stepped down and turned to where I could see his face. It was the gentleman from the flatboat. Elder Hyde.

I commenced to holler, "Poppy, look!" but he was nowhere in my sight. The folks close up jostled and pushed at each other, some wanting to ask questions and others ready to get on with business. Standing on tiptoe, I tried to see over the forest of people, but I couldn't. I turned every which way hoping to catch sight of Poppy, but it seemed he'd been swallowed up. Just as fear started settling over me, I heard someone calling my name.

"Hannah! Over here, dear!"

I spun around to find Mrs. Dalton coming toward me.

"Mrs. Dalton, I can't find my pa," I said loud. "He was right here with me, and now he's gone!"

She nodded her head. "I know, dear. Let's go back to my place."

"What do you mean, you know?" I said, following her down the road.

"I closed the store for just a minute to come hear the elders. When I saw your pa in the crowd, he asked if I'd look after you for a while."

I was relieved to know Poppy hadn't truly disappeared.

"Mrs. Dalton," I said, "who are those men—the elders?"

"They're missionaries from a church called the Mormons. I've enjoyed listening to them before. But some folks around here don't like them in town. I can't see why. It appears to be a decent, wholesome religion. I don't know what it is, but there's just something about them."

"That's what my pa said too," I mumbled.

Poppy came in a short while after us. Said he stayed behind to chat with the elders a bit. But they were so covered with people asking questions that he never got near them. On our way up to the room, he talked so fast, I didn't hardly know who he was. His face seemed all lit up, and he even moved different, somehow.

He talked all excited and fast, like a child, saying, "I think those men have it, Hannah. They answered some of the questions I've had for years. And they knew the Bible a far sight better than most preachers. All my life, I've been looking, and now it could be right here, this close."

Finally he looked into my face and saw that I didn't know what he was rambling about. Leaning forward in his chair, he said, "The truth, Hannah.

I think these men have the truth we've been hunting for."

CHAPTER NINE

A Purse of Gold

My pa didn't sleep much that night. He sat at the table searching through Mrs. Dalton's Bible or pacing around the room. A few times I even saw him praying.

Close to midnight I whispered, "Poppy, are you all right?"

"Yes, girl," he said. "Just have plenty to sort out, is all. There's a peculiar, restless feeling gnawing away at me."

"You haven't laid down once yet, have you?"

"Doesn't seem to be much sleep in me, just confusion, mostly. But don't you fret now. I'll be fine."

Pulling the blankets up under my chin, I curled around and shut my eyes.

By daylight I s'posed he'd be downstairs getting gathered for home. But not knowing when he'd finally gone to sleep, I figured to leave him be. Now and again he'd toss and turn, mumbling low to himself. It was worrisome to see him this way.

I sat at the table fingering my parcel. Part of me wanted to tear the brown wrapping off and have another look at the pretty things inside, but the other part wanted to take the package home all tied up and new. I thought on the gifts—Ma's looking glass, Sophie's magnifier, Cally's rag doll, and the stockings. Why, Poppy even had himself a watch. What Ma said was true. We were bringing home treasure, sure enough.

I glanced over again at Poppy. He looked so troubled, even for a man sound asleep. The worst part was that in all my life, I can't recall ever seeing him act confused about anything. Until last night, that is. I wished to help him. But what was there to do?

The thought struck me then that if trying to find the Lord's truth was causing Poppy to be this way, then maybe the Lord could help him find it, and feel better.

I pushed the chair aside and knelt down by it. In a quiet voice I said, "Oh Lord, my pa surely needs your help. You know he's been hunting answers for a long, long time. I love him, and I'd do anything to help him be all right. But I can't figure how. So, I'm asking you to show us the way, so's he can find peace. Thank you kindly. In Jesus' name. Amen."

Poppy looked the same, but I felt better.

With no warning, he sat up.

"Hannah?"

"Yes, Poppy?"

"I know what we're to do. But I need your help."

I sat on the side of his bed.

"Take my coin bag and find the elders. There's a message I want you to read and give them, along with the money."

I shot a surprised look at him and wondered if he had a fever. "But, Poppy, why? What about our supplies and the house and . . ."

He held up his hand. "Hannah, don't ask questions now. Do what I say."

I was left to wonder what was happening. Whether or not I understood, it's a right thing to obey your pa. So I took the folded paper and the bag off the table. It was heavy and jingled like a pile of log chains.* Knowing its worth, I felt afraid to just drop it in my pocket or hold it in my hand—so I did both at the same time.

Wondering what would happen when we came home with no money, I turned to him. "Are you sure, Poppy? All this money?"

He looked so weary, but he nodded for me to go.

I passed Mrs. Dalton in the hall. How I ached to ask her if I was doing the right thing. But I figured she'd never make sense of it. I knew I couldn't.

She smiled and asked, "Did you sleep well, dear?"

"Mostly, ma'am."

"I'm pleased to hear that."

Before she turned down the hall, I got brave and said, "Mrs. Dalton? Would you know where I can find the gentlemen who were preaching yesterday?"

"Well, I heard a customer say they took lodging just down the street at Owens' Inn. Mr. Owens is always taking in preachers."

I made my way to the door. Turning the knob, I said, "Thank you, ma'am," and went out to the street.

Lucky for me, the inn was only a few buildings past the mercantile. As I walked up the steps, out came the very man I was looking for, alongside a few other men. They went right past me and started down the stairs.

I cleared my throat and said, "Excuse me, sir?"

The rest of the men kept talking, but the preacher turned around.

"Yes, miss? May I help you?"

He smiled like a regular neighbor from home, though it was plain from his dress that he was a fancy gentleman. His looks were friendly and more pleasant than most men of religion. Some I've seen wear such stern, angry puckers, it's hard to tell if they battle the devil, or fiddle with him.

Stepping up, I pulled the coin bag from my pocket and held it out with both hands.

"Ma may fix our flint,* but Pa says I'm to give you this. So I'll be proud to mind him."

His face was near shining as he took the bag. "Bless you, child," he said, "and your father as well. Bless you."

I turned to leave, then remembered the message and said, "Oh, and sir?"

He was still there, looking amazed.

"My pa said to tell you he'd be obliged if you'd put a mind to him when you pray in the Holy Land."

"Who is your father, child? May I not thank him personally?"

"I wasn't to say, sir."

"Please, tell your father that Elder Orson Hyde sends his deepest gratitude. The blessings of the Lord shall be upon him. Neither he nor his family shall feel a loss from this sacrifice." He reached into his pocket and added, "Give him this."

He held out a book to me. I took it. That was as far as my bravery went, so I ran back to the hotel.

Coming into the store, I saw the shelf of books. 'Cept for the Bible, most folks I know don't own any. "They're a costly 'stravagance,"* Ma says. Looking at the one in my hand, all I could think of was our supplies, the nails, and four rooms instead of two.

I pondered on it only a minute, then said, "Mrs. Dalton, how much do you expect this book is worth?"

"Well, dear," she said, "I don't know. I'd have to look into it. Books are quite expensive."

I gave it to her. She thumbed through it and turned it in her hands. "The Book of Mormon," she said. "Hannah, did the elders give you this?"

I nodded. "Do you think we could get the supplies we need in trade? Salt, sugar, flour, and nails?"

"Well, I've wanted to read it. I suppose I could . . ."

"I have this too," I said, handing her the six coins she'd given me just yesterday.

"I'll have a boy load the supplies into your wagon."

As I headed up the stairs, the oddest feeling went through me. Like a voice was telling me, "No!" Was this a mistake? With all my might, I pushed the thought away.

As I came into our room, there sat Poppy, not only up and dressed, but whistling.

"Feeling better, Poppy?"

"Hannah, I'll tell you. I've been wrestling with this like a wild animal since yesterday. Then, from the second you left this room, I've had a peaceful feeling fill me. I don't know how, but my heart tells me these men have something that will lead us to the truth."

Like a flash of lightning I heard the words of

Poppy's prayer come into my mind, from that morning a while back. "Bless us," he'd said, "that we'll live to find your truth and *feel peace and contentment on that day.*" It gave me goose prickles up my arms.

Poppy stood up, saying, "I want to talk to them before we go home. I can't shake the idea that they have something for us."

I felt sick. The book. That's what he was feeling. The book I traded away was what Poppy'd been looking for all this time. The supplies would already be loaded in the wagon by now, and I couldn't think how we'd face Ma without them. There had to be a way to fanangle that book back. Staring down at the floor, I had an idea, but I didn't like it much. Snatching my parcel off the table, I made for the door, saying, "Be right back. There's one last thing that needs doing."

I ran downstairs and up to the counter. With barely any breath left, I said, "Mrs. Dalton, would you consider taking my parcel in trade for the book I just gave you?"

She tipped her head and looked into my eyes, like I had me a blue face. "Hannah, I don't understand. These are the gifts for your family. Why would you . . . ?"

"It's real important, ma'am."

She sighed. "Of course, dear. Here's your book. Though I'm a bit confused."

"I know, ma'am. You and me together."

CHAPTER TEN

Filled Basket

Poppy wasted no time thinking about how the book got to my hands. Carefully taking it from me, he acted like he had a hold of some fragile hatchling.* His face took on a calm sweetness like I'd never seen before. I thought for just one minute about having to give up my treasures, but there wasn't as much pain to it as I expected.

Poppy and I took turns reading to each other until the candle burned low.

It seems that a long, long time ago, a man named Nephi and his family ran away from Jerusalem 'cause their neighbors were getting ornery. Nephi's father tried to interest them in behaving, but they didn't like that neither. So, even though the family was rich, they left behind everything they had claim to and moved out to the prairie.

"Quite a story," said Poppy, lost in thought.

"Would you ever do that, Poppy?" I asked.

"Do what?"

"Move away from your home 'cause the Lord told you so?"

Poppy thought on that for a few minutes.

"Well, Hannah," he said, "hearing the Lord's words and *doing* what he tells you are mighty different things. Most everyone can hear, but some folks find the doing to be more than they can muster. Your ma and I been praying and listening hard to know the truth for a long time now. I reckon we'd do whatever He asked so's we could find it."

I held up the Book of Mormon and said, "Is this the truth, Poppy?"

"I hope so, girl. Feels like it to me."

"So if He told us to leave everything and head somewhere else . . . we'd do it?" I asked.

"It's a sacrifice we'd be proud to make, and trust the Lord to get us by."

"Hmmm. That's what Sophie says about sacrifices. And you know Sophie's always right."

It didn't take us a full six days to make it back home, with the wagon empty and all. Poppy and I started singing at the top of our lungs about half a mile from our place. Old Harley started howling and yapping from the yard long before we could see the house. I thought Farish would hurt himself, scrambling up the hill the way he did. As we made the last turn, down the path toward us came Ma, with baby Lark, and Sophie hanging on tight to Cally's dress. I couldn't help laughing to myself at the thought of Sophie letting go.

Poppy slowed enough so's I could jump off and run to Ma and my sisters. All of us talked and hugged at the same time while walking up to the house. Ma handed Lark to me and ran to the barn so she could throw her arms around Poppy.

Once inside, we sat close to the fire and chattered like a bunch of magpies. Cally kept tugging at me, till finally I looked at her and said, "What is it, baby?"

She grinned wide so I could see she'd lost two teeth while we were gone.

"Where's our presents?" she asked.

I couldn't think of the right way to tell her there weren't any. Though I knew he couldn't help me, for some reason I looked over to Poppy. But before I could answer, Ma took a hold of his hand.

"Yes," she said. "Let's bring in the supplies. I'll have apple tarts made by breakfast."

"Well, now," Poppy said, "we just may have a problem. Haddy, here's how it is . . ."

I smiled and said, "It's fine, Poppy. The supplies are up front under the canvas. Flour, sugar, salt, and nails."

"Well, I'll be skinned," he said. "I wondered why that old cover looked so bulky."

"But where are my presents?" Cally whined.

"Cally," I said, "here's how it is . . ."

"It's fine, Hannah. Your gifts are under the seat in the wagon. It wasn't easy to keep you from finding them, neither."

"Now, wait," I said. "How'd you know about my parcel?"

"Mrs. Dalton gave me a few hints. And it didn't take too much to buy it back. So we made out like a couple of horse thieves, wouldn't you say?"

"How'd you do it, Poppy? You didn't have no money."

He smiled.

Ma and the girls sat staring at us. I could tell

they were lost in the woods.* I couldn't see how he bought back my parcel, 'cause I knew he'd given his money to those Mormon elders. Poppy was still grinning.

Suddenly I knew. He sold his watch! When he saw that I'd caught on, he put a finger to his lips, so I wouldn't say nothing. I just shook my head.

Ma stood up. "I'm ready to know what you two are talking about. Did you bring supplies home or not? And how's this about you having no money? Why, you should have a full coin bag."

Poppy said, "Ma, I think it's time that you and me went for a walk. I'll explain while unloading the wagon."

When next I saw Ma and Poppy, he was hugging on to her and she was holding the preacher's book, crying for all she was worth. It was the best kind of cry, though. I could tell. At last they had the truth in sight, and I could see that her heart was near bursting with joy.

After Poppy came in from unloading the wagon, the gifts were shared and the supplies put away. At last he sat back in the rocker to rest. Cally snuggled up on his lap, holding her dolly and wearing her new foot warmers—on her *arms*.

I tried my best to give Sophie the story of our money, but she didn't seem to be worried at all.

"It's right this way, Hannah," she said. "We don't need it now. We're not hiring a boy, come spring. See, we have a surprise for you too. While you and Poppy were gone we got us some company."

I must have had confusion all over my face, but she just giggled and nodded to Ma.

"Uncle Wade," Ma said. "He's come back to stay. City life don't suit him, so he bought his old cabin back. Says he'll be here to help add to our place. There's no reason to fret over the money."

It was then I remembered the words Elder Hyde had used.

I said, "'Neither he nor his family shall feel a loss from this sacrifice.'"

"What?" Sophie asked.

"I was just recalling some words about sacrifice. Poppy and I've given away more in the last week than we've ever seen before. But in the end, the Lord saw to it that we didn't lose nothing at all."

Ma set her hand on our new book of scriptures. "Truly, Hannah," Ma said, "you've brought us back the greatest treasure of all. The truth."

My sister told me this would feel mighty good.
And you know—Sophie is always right.

GLOSSARY
In Hannah's Own Words

apple butter—A preserve that looks and tastes just like applesauce, only thicker. It's mighty good on bread too. See page 24.

apple rings—First Ma cuts the center out of the apple. Then she slices it into thin pieces with the core hole in the middle. We run a thread through it and hang it to dry. See page 24.

ashcake—A simple corn bread baked in the ashes. See page 43.

big time—Having a lot of pure fun. See page 16.

bitterroot—The undergrowth of a small plant used for medicine. It tastes real bad, so to get someone to take a dose is like dragging a mule. See page 23.

blood tonic—A tea used to help tone up the body and refresh the spirit. We mostly drink it in the spring to thin the blood. Ma makes tonic for our family out of sassafras, spicebush, or sweet birch. Even with honey stirred in, tonic is nasty. See page 13.

blue streak—I meant that Papa was talking real fast and had a lot to say. See page 41.

came on—When fruits and vegetables come on it's another way of saying it is their season to ripen up. See page 16.

cider—Apple juice made from running fruit through a press. It's used for drinking, flavoring, or as vinegar. See page 24.

constitution—The way a person is put together. Ma was worried about the baby getting sick. See page 12.

coon hunting—Whenever our dogs Harley and Farish had chased a raccoon up a tree, they would take to barking and carrying on as if the world were coming to an end. See page 10.

crackling bread—When hog fat is boiled down, the little bits of pork left at the bottom of the kettle are called cracklins. Ma uses them in breads and biscuits. See page 31.

cushaw pie—Cushaw is a vegetable a lot like a pumpkin or squash. Ma cooks and mashes it, adds some spices, and from that she makes the best pies you'd ever eat. See page 31.

deerskin cover—A deer hide nailed over the window to keep out the cold and light. See page 30.

dock seeds—My sisters and I just love to chew on seeds of the dock plant. It is a knee-high weed with crinkly leaves. The seeds are dark brown and crunchy. See page 31.

fancied—Thought on something or wanted it a lot. See page 45.

fatback—The fat and fat meat from the upper side of a pig. See page 6.

felling trees—Chopping down trees. See page 17.

fix our flint—One way of saying we'd be in big trouble. See page 64.

flatboat—A large raft used to carry wagons, livestock, people, and their belongings down a river. See page 37.

flax—A long, thin plant with blue flowers. We use it to make linen cloth. See page 21.

flintlock—My poppy's hunting rifle is called a flintlock because it uses flint to set off the firing charge. See page 17.

full chisel—Very fast. See page 54.

guide pole—A long pole used to guide the flatboat down the river. It works like a large oar. See page 39.

hard winter—In the mountains we have many ways to tell if a long, cold winter is coming. One way to tell is if the cows turn up with a split in their hoof. See page 7.

hatchling—A new baby chick. See page 69.

honeycomb—The wax made by bees. It is full of holes which the bees use to store honey and their eggs. See page 14.

Job's turkey—Job was a man in the Bible who lost everything and ended up poor and sad. I figure Job's turkey would have even less that *he* did. See page 1.

kin—Anyone who is part of your family is kin. See page 16.

large-ended ladies—Well-dressed women wore contraptions called bustles that gave them the appearance of having hourglass-figures. See page 53.

leave off—To never leave off means to never forget to do something. See page 2.

lind—Our name for the big, shady linden tree, also called basswood. See page 34.

linsey-woolsey—A rough, scratchy cloth made from linen and wool. See page 26.

log chains—A set of long, sturdy chains used to haul trees from the forest. See page 63.

looking glass—A reflector, or mirror. See page 47.

lost in the woods—When someone doesn't know what you're talking about. See pages 72–73.

milking—The batch we get from one morning of milking the cows. See page 5.

minding Cally—Ma meant baby-sitting our little sister. See page 12.

morel—A sponge mushroom that grows mostly under apple trees. The best time to hunt them is after a warm rain, when the dark blue violets bloom. See page 16.

mobcap—A soft, linen cap worn mostly inside the house. See page 18.

new moon—When the moon cannot be seen or when it is just a tiny slice in the sky. See page 14.

GLOSSARY

night noise—The creatures that fill up the night with their chirping, hooting, and chatter make what we call the night noises. See page 32.

odorous—When something smells so bad you have to move to some fresh air. See page 12.

pinched back—Poppy held tight to the horses' reins to keep them from moving ahead too fast. See page 44.

pine—To long for or to wish for something so bad your insides ache. See page 8.

poke—A tall, pretty plant with white flowers and dark red berries. Folks around here cook the leaves and stems for food. Don't never use the berries or roots for eating though, 'cause they are poison. See page 13.

potato pounder—A carved, polished, wooden stick with a flat end. It is used for smashing up any cooked fruit or vegetables, especially potatoes. See page 47.

pull off—Take the flatboat to the side bank. See page 39.

ramps—A plant that looks a lot like a lily. It grows from a small bulb that looks like a clove of garlic. Some people love them in stews or fried, but most folks don't even want them in the yard because they smell so poorly. See page 6.

robbing beehives—Taking most of the honey out of the beehives. See page 14.

GLOSSARY

root it out—Search out and find where something is hiding. See page 7.

rousing—What someone does to get another person to wake up or get moving. Some people call out, others give a person a hard shake. Our ma uses a broom handle and taps on our bedroom floor from underneath it. See page 17.

shift—An underslip with short sleeves. See page 25.

shoepacs—My shoes look a lot like the moccasins the Indians wear, but they come to the ankles and have a sturdy sole. In the wintertime we fill the bottoms with dry leaves or deer hair to keep our feet warm. See page 43.

slaughtering season—Towards the end of November or when the weather turns cold to stay is the perfect time to kill and cure pork. It needs to be near freezing outside to keep the meat from spoiling while it cures. See page 9.

sourwood trees—Tall, bushy trees with crooked trunks. The leaves are good to chew as a thirst quencher. In the summertime these trees are covered with tiny, white flowers that the bees just go crazy over. If you stand under a sourwood in July, you'll think the whole tree is singing. But it's just the hum of a million bees. See page 15.

split hoof—A cow's hoof is a bit like our fingernails, only a sight bigger. Towards fall, if a cow ends up with a split in the hoof, Poppy believes it's a sure way to predict that a very cold winter is coming soon. See page 7.

spoiled—My cap had become crumpled up and dirty from being worn every day. See page 44.

'stravagance—Something wonderful that we didn't need at all. See page 65.

strawbag—A wool, drawstring bag filled with straw to keep eggs cool and safe from cracking. See page 33.

stringing up—We take a needle and thread and sew through apple slices or whole morel. Next we tie the strings in loops and hang them up on the warm fireplace bricks to dry. See page 24.

stroke—When I said "I about took a stroke," my meaning was that it scared me so bad my heart nearly stopped. See page 30.

tainted—If something spoiled or bad tasting gets into food or drink, we say it is tainted, or ruined. See page 6.

take to—To really take a liking to something or enjoy it. See page 45.

tin grater—A flat piece of metal with nail holes driven into it. We use the rough side to grind corn or other grain into meal. See page 24.

tonic—A drink meant to better a person's health. Most folks don't take to them much though, because tonics usually taste real nasty. See page 6.

too dear—We mean something costs too high a price. It's expensive. See page 48.

twists—Sticks and rags twisted together and lit on fire. See page 14.

upbringing—The way a person is raised, or taught at home. See page 26.

vegetables buried—In the fall, Poppy digs a deep hole, lines it with straw, and buries the fruits and vegetables for us to use come winter. This keeps the apples, carrots, potatoes, etc., from freezing. See page 25.

waxed rags—When Ma bottles jam, she tops it with melted wax. She dips a small piece of cloth into the wax and ties it around the top of the jar. That way, the jam is sealed and the top stays clean. See page 36.

wink—Faster than anything. See page 41.

wool drawers—Long under-britches made out of light wool. See page 25.

wrapping cloak—A long, woven shawl made to keep a whole body warm. See page 26.

yarbs—Plants and herbs. See page 13.

What Really Happened

While preaching at a public meeting in Philadelphia in 1840, Elder Orson Hyde mentioned his mission call to Jerusalem, and that Mormon missionaries travel without any money. After his speech, an unknown person delivered a purse of gold to him. This generous donor asked only that Elder Hyde remember to mention him in prayer when he reached the Holy Land.

Upon Elder Hyde's arrival in Israel, he went to the Mount of Olives and offered his prayer of dedication to the Lord. Among other things, he said, "Particularly do Thou bless the stranger in Philadelphia, whom I never saw, but who sent me gold, with a request that I should pray for him in Jerusalem. Now, O Lord, let blessings come upon him from an unexpected quarter, and let his basket be filled, and his storehouse abound with plenty."

It was later revealed that Joseph Ellison Beck had been the generous "stranger." His son, John F. Beck, said of his father's blessing:

"We settled in Spanish Fork [Utah] where . . . father died at the age of ninety-three, having enjoyed good health until within three days of his death. I do not know of an apostate among any of father's posterity. He always had plenty for his family and loaned breadstuffs to scores who were in want. He did not become rich, but always had money laid aside for a time of need."

The author is proud to be one of the great-great-granddaughters of Joseph Ellison Beck, and pleased to honor his good name in this fictitious tale.

L. K. Anderson

ABOUT THE AUTHOR

 Launi K. Anderson grew up in Los Angeles and San Diego, California. After moving to Utah, she worked at Deseret Book stores in Salt Lake City and Orem for four years, including a year as a children's book buyer. She loves historical fiction and enjoys the research as much as the writing.

Launi lives in Orem, Utah, with her husband, Devon, and their three daughters and two sons. She loves music and spends some of her happiest hours listening to her husband and children play the piano, violin, and flute. Her hobbies include flower gardening and collecting creamers and great quotes. Her favorite things are history, cats, family, parties, people, and the sound of wind chimes. In her ward, she has served in the Primary, Young Women, and Relief Society and is currently second counselor in the Primary presidency.

She is the author of five other Latter-day Daughters books: *Clarissa's Crossing, Maren's Hope, Ellie's Gold, Violet's Garden,* and *Gracie's Angel.*

From *Catherine's Remembrance*
Another Exciting New Title
in the Latter-day Daughters Series

Pa helped the oxen pull the wagon onto the barge, then he unhooked them and tied them with a short rope to the barge bottom. The wagon was lashed down so it wouldn't move. The wheels were locked with a long stick. The rest of our animals were tied so they wouldn't bolt. Ma and I walked onto the barge last. I clutched at her hand.

"Look, Ma," I said, pointing out into the deeper, fast-moving part of the river. Large chunks of ice rode the waves of the Mississippi. Our barge moved out further from the shore, caught the current, and swung out wide.

I screamed without meaning to. The sound of the water seemed to rage in my ears. "Oh, no, Ma," I said. I pointed at a chunk of ice that moved swiftly from upriver. "It's going to hit us!"

The ice crashed into the side of the barge, making a loud thud. *We're going to crash apart,* I thought. But I couldn't make my mouth say the words.